For the children of Makindu, Kenya,
and for all my fellow 2008 Proper Walkers

In loving memory of all the good dogs, especially Cocoa

Henry Holt and Company, LLC
Publishers since 1866
175 Fifth Avenue
New York, New York 10010
www.HenryHoltKids.com

Library of Congress Cataloging-in-Publication Data
Wolff, Ashley.
When Lucy goes out walking : a puppy's first year / Ashley Wolff. — 1st ed.
p.   cm.
"Christy Ottaviano Books."
Summary: A curious puppy enjoys an adventure in each month of her first year.
ISBN 978-0-8050-8168-8
[1. Stories in rhyme. 2. Dogs—Fiction. 3. Animals—Infancy—Fiction.
4. Months—Fiction. 5. Year—Fiction.] I. Title.
PZ8.3.W843Whe 2009   [E]—dc22   2008038226

First Edition—2009 / Designed by Véronique Lefèvre Sweet
The artist used gouache on Arches Cover to create the illustrations for this book.
Printed in May 2009 in China by South China Printing Company Ltd., Dongguan City,
Guangdong Province, on acid-free paper. ∞

3 5 7 9 10 8 6 4 2

When Lucy Goes Out Walking

A Puppy's First Year

Ashley Wolff

Christy Ottaviano Books

HENRY HOLT AND COMPANY ✦ NEW YORK

December

January

When Lucy goes out walking
In January snows,
She leaves a trail of puppy prints
Everywhere she goes.
"Frosty fur!
Brrr, Brrr, Brrr!"
In January snows.

January

February

When Lucy goes out walking
In February's chill,
She joins a crowd of children
Racing down the hill.
"Hurry! Fast!
Don't be last!"
In February's chill.

March

February

March

When Lucy goes out walking
In March's misty fog,
She sniffs and meets, wags and greets
Each and every dog.
"Romp and run!
Let's have some fun!"
In March's misty fog.

April

April

When Lucy goes out walking
The April wind blows cold.
Breezes lift the zooming kites—
Purple, red, and gold!
"Dive and swoop!
Loop the loop!"
The April wind blows cold.

May

When Lucy goes out walking
In flower-spangled May,
This grassy field's a perfect place
To frolic in today.
"Come roll over!
Smell the clover!"
In flower-spangled May.

June

When Lucy goes out walking
One afternoon in June,
A storm is coming from the west—
She hears the thunder BOOM!
"Time to hide!
Safe inside!"
One afternoon in June.

July

When Lucy goes out walking
One hot night in July,
She stretches on the grassy hill
Beneath a glittering sky.
"I see Mars!
Shooting stars!"
One hot night in July.

August

When Lucy goes out walking
In August's muggy heat,
The neighbor cats all scatter
Up and down the street.
"To and fro!
Where'd they go?"
In August's muggy heat.

September

August

September

When Lucy goes out walking
One warm September day,
She pauses at the playground
And hears the children say,
"What's your name?
Come join our game!"
One warm September day.

October

September

October

When Lucy goes out walking
Beneath October's trees,
Leaves dress up the sidewalk,
Right up to her knees.
"Colors scatter!
Squirrels chatter!"
Beneath October's trees.

November

October

November

When Lucy goes out walking
In cold November rain,
She wears her cozy winter coat
While splashing down the lane.
"Puddles slosh!
Oh my gosh!"
In cold November rain.

December

When Lucy goes out walking
In first December snows,
She leaves a trail of big dog prints
Everywhere she goes.
"I'm not a pup!
I'm all grown up!"
In first December snows!